Richard F   ddiment

Happy Birthday, Bear

ALISON
GREEN
BOOKS

Bear woke up and yawned and scratched his head.
There was something special about today,
but he couldn't think what it was. Suddenly
he remembered. It was his birthday!

"If it's my birthday, I'd better have a party,"
he said, jumping up.
"What will I need?

Balloons . . .

and friends . . .

and presents.

Bears love
presents!"

Bear wrote invitations to his three
best friends, the beaver, the wild boar
and the heron:

PLEASE COME TO BEAR'S
BIRTHDAY PARTY
FOUR O'CLOCK
AT THE BEARCAVE.
GAMES AND FOOD.

P.S. BEARS LOVE PRESENTS!!!

Then he folded the invitations
and hurried out to deliver them.

Later that afternoon, Bear waited impatiently for his guests –

and his presents – to arrive.

"Happy Birthday!" called his friends, as they came up the path.

"We've got you some presents."

"Oh, thank you," said Bear.

"I wasn't expecting any."

"Open mine first!" cried the heron.

"No, mine," grunted the boar.

"No, mine!" squeaked the beaver . . .

"Here!

"Take the parcel, shake the parcel,
Wiggle it and spin it,
Rattle it and sniff at it,
And try to guess what's in it."

Bear shook the parcel. It made a scratchy sound.

He tore the wrapping paper.

There was a box inside.

And in the box he found . . .

"Sticks?" said Bear. He was disappointed.

"Sticks are good," replied the beaver. "I built my house out of sticks."

"I think they're a silly present," said Bear, and he put the parcel down.

"You'll like my present!" said the wild boar:

"Take the parcel, shake the parcel,
Wiggle it and spin it,
Rattle it and sniff at it,
And try to guess what's in it."

Bear wiggled the parcel.
It made a slurping sound.
He tore the wrapping paper.
There was a box inside.

And in the box he found . . .

"Mud?" said Bear. He was very disappointed.
"Mud's good," replied the boar. "You can snuffle in mud."

"Mud's even sillier than sticks!" said Bear, and
he dropped the parcel on the floor.

The last present was the heron's.

"Take the parcel, shake the parcel,
Wiggle it and spin it,
Rattle it and sniff at it,
And try to guess what's in it."

Bear rattled the parcel.
It made a clacking sound.
He tore the wrapping paper.
There was a box inside.
And in the box he found . . .

"Stones?" said Bear.

Now he was really disappointed.

"Stones are good," said the heron. "You can stand on them
when you're fishing and keep your feet dry."
"Stones are even sillier than mud!" sniffed Bear,
and he threw the parcel into a corner.

"These are the worst
presents I've ever had," he said.
"I don't want a party any more.
You can all go home!"

Next morning, Bear decided
to get rid of his silly presents. He walked
into the forest to throw the sticks away.
They rattled against tree trunks as he went:

rattly tattly tat!

Bear liked that noise.
He rattled more trunks, and more.

He found a hollow log and began to drum on it, singing:

"Rattly tat, tum tum,
Rattly tattly tum,
Bear loves thumping,
Thumping on a drum."

And he liked drumming
so much that he decided to
keep the drumsticks after all.

"The beaver was right," he said when he got back home. "Sticks are a good present. But mud isn't."

He took the box outside and emptied it on the ground:

squelch!

Bear liked that noise.
He trod in the mud and squelched it louder.
He jumped up and down, singing:

"Squilch squelch squilch squelch,
Squilching on the ground,
Bear loves squilching,
Squelching all around!"

And he liked squelching so much that he decided
to scoop the mud back into the box and keep it.

"The boar was right," he said. "Mud isn't a silly present either. But stones are."

So he took the stones the heron had given him and went down to the lake to sink them. He threw the first stone high into the air, and watched it fall into the water:

splosh!

Bear liked that noise. He sploshed another stone, and another, singing:

"Splish splosh splish splosh,
Water splishing high,
Bear loves sploshing,
Making water fly!"

And he liked sploshing so much
that he kept some stones
to play with later.

Sticks, mud, stones: they were wonderful presents.

Bear felt so bad about how he'd behaved at the party.

How could he show he was sorry?

Later that day, his friends were talking by the lakeside, when Bear came hurrying up.

"I'm so happy to see you!" he called. "Those presents you gave me were the best I've ever had!"

"The sticks?" asked the beaver.

"The mud?" asked the boar.

"The stones?" asked the heron.

"I like them all!" said Bear.
"And I've got you some presents
to make up. Come with me!"

Back in the bearcave, there were three presents waiting. Bear smiled:

"Take the parcels, shake the parcels,
Wiggle them and spin them,
Rattle them and sniff at them
And try to guess what's in them."

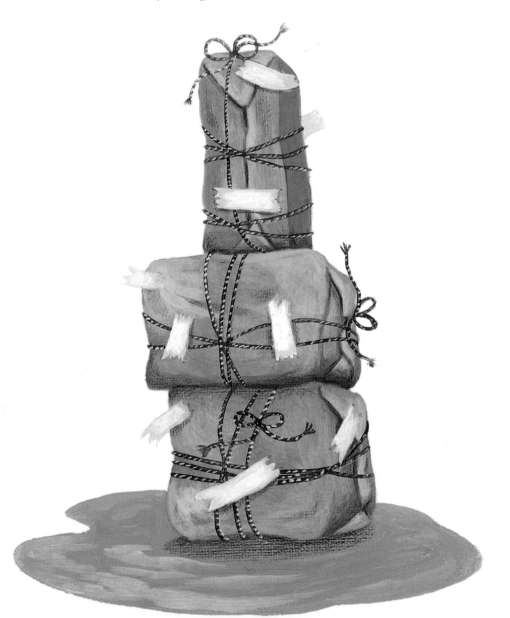

His friends shook and wiggled
and rattled their presents.

They tore the
wrapping paper.

There were boxes inside.
And when they opened the
boxes they found . . .

"Honeycomb!" said the beaver.
"Mmm!" said the others.
And at last they had their party. They nibbled
and snuffled and pecked greedily until all
the honey had gone.

Then Bear took his friends outside to show them . . .

. . . drumming: Rattly tat tum tum!

Squelching: Squilch squelch,
squilch squelch!

And sploshing:

Splish splosh, splish splosh,

Splish splosh,

Splish!

For my mum – C.L.

First published in 2008 by Alison Green Books
An imprint of Scholastic Children's Books
Euston House, 24 Eversholt Street
London NW1 1DB
A division of Scholastic Ltd
www.scholastic.co.uk
London – New York – Toronto – Sydney – Auckland
Mexico City – New Delhi – Hong Kong

Text copyright © 2008 Richard Edwards
Illustrations copyright © 2008 Carol Liddiment

HB ISBN: 978 1 407103 63 1
PB ISBN: 978 0 439944 38 0

1 3 5 7 9 8 6 4 2
The moral rights of the author and illustrator have been asserted.

Papers used by Scholastic Children's Books are made from wood grown in sustainable forests.